Grandma's Saturday Soup

Grandma's Saturday Soup

Written by Sally Fraser

Illustrated by Derek Brazell

Jamaican Patois translation by Roy Lee

Monday mornin' Mummy wake me early.
"Get up Mimi and get dressed fi school."
I climb out a de bed all sleepy and tired,
and pull back de curtains.

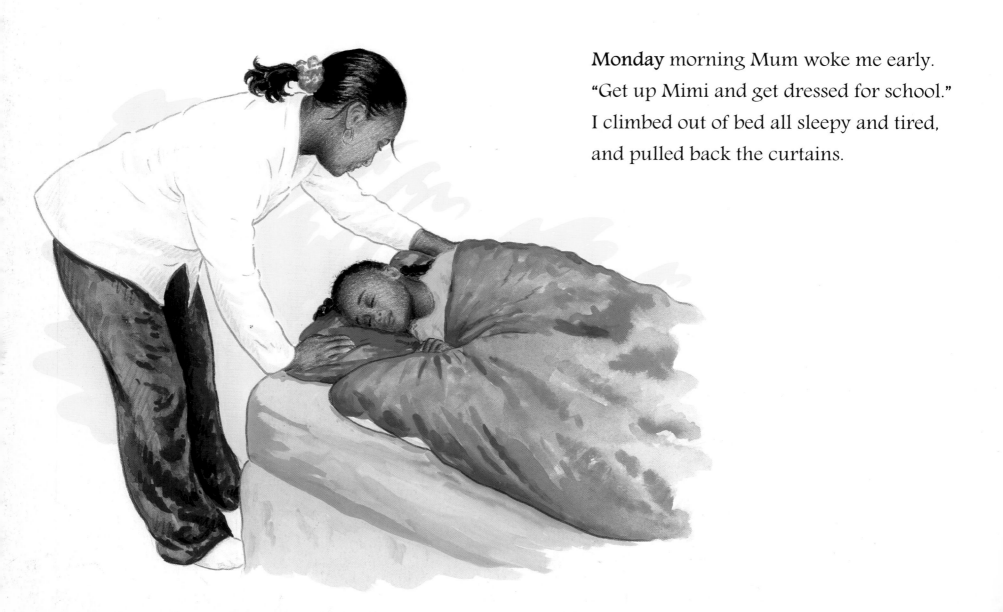

Monday morning Mum woke me early.
"Get up Mimi and get dressed for school."
I climbed out of bed all sleepy and tired,
and pulled back the curtains.

De mornin' was cloudy and cold.
De clouds in the sky were white and fluffy.
Dem remind me of the dumplings inna
Grandma's Saturday Soup.

The morning was cloudy and cold.

The clouds in the sky were white and fluffy.

They reminded me of the dumplings in Grandma's Saturday Soup.

Grandma tells me stories about Jamaica when I go to her house.

Grandma tells me stories about Jamaica when I go to her house.

"De clouds in Jamaica bring the 'eaviest rain.
It's like summadi turn on de tap inna de sky.
De warm breeze come now and move dem on
and de sun comes out again."

"The clouds in Jamaica bring the heaviest rain.

It's like someone has turned the tap on in the sky.

The warm breeze moves them on and the sun comes out again."

Tuesday mornin' Daddy tek me go a school.
De day was cold and crisp; as it did snow de night before.

Tuesday morning Dad took me to school.
The day was cold and crisp; it had snowed in the night.

It's white and smooth and looks like the inside of a sliced yam.
Jus' like de yam inna Grandma's Saturday Soup.

It's white and smooth and looked like the inside of a sliced yam.

Just like the yam in Grandma's Saturday Soup.

Grandma tell me dat de white powdery sand on de beach looks like fresh snow but it's never cold.

Grandma tells me that the white powdery sand on the beaches looks like fresh snow but it's never cold.

I wonder if I could mek a sandman wid de white sand?
Wouldn't dat be funny?!

I wonder if I could make a sandman with the white sand?
Wouldn't that be funny?!

Wednesday the snow fell harder. It was
cold but I was wrapped up warm.
*Grandma again tells me stories about
Jamaica when I go to her house.*

Wednesday the snow fell harder. It was cold but I was wrapped up warm.

Grandma tells me stories about Jamaica when I go to her house.

"De sun shines every day. De sun is warm on yu skin and yu only need to wear yur shorts an' a t-shirt."
Warm every day? Shorts and t-shirt? Me cyaant believe dat.

"The sun shines every day. The sun is warm on your skin and you only need to wear your shorts and a T-shirt."
Warm every day? Shorts and T-shirt? I can't believe that.

At afternoon play we mek snowballs
and throw dem at each other.

At afternoon play we made snowballs
and threw them at each other.

The snowballs remind me of the round soft potatoes in Grandma's Saturday Soup.

De snowballs remind me of de round soft potatoes inna Grandma's Saturday Soup.

On Thursday I went to de library after school
with my friend Layla and her mummy.

On **Thursday** I went to the library
after school with my friend Layla
and her Mum.

As we pass de park we see de likkle bulbs a start fi grow. De likkle green shoots a poke through de snow. Dem look like de spring onions inna Grandma's Saturday Soup.

As we passed the park we saw the little bulbs starting to grow. The little green shoots poked through the snow. They looked like the spring onions in Grandma's Saturday Soup.

Grandma tells me about the wonderful plants and flowers in Jamaica.
"In Jamaica the most beautiful flowers grow wild.
They are all different colours and sizes
and their smell fills the air."
I've never seen flowers like that before,
I wonder if she's only joking?

Grandma tells me about the wonderful plants and
flowers inna Jamaica.
"Inna Jamaica de most beautiful flowers grow wild.
Alla dem have all kinda different colours
and sizes, and de smell fills the air."
I've never seen flowers like dat before.
I wonder if she's joking wid me?

On Friday Mummy and Daddy are late fi work.
"Hurry Mimi, choose a piece a fruit to tek to school."

On **Friday** Mum and Dad are late for work.

"Hurry Mimi, choose a piece of fruit to take to school."

I looked at de bowl full of fruit.
Should I choose an orange, an apple or a pear?
De apple and pear; fi dem colour and shape reminded me
of the cho-cho inna Grandma's Saturday Soup.

I looked at the bowl full of fruit.

Should I choose an orange, an apple or a pear?

The apple and pear; their colour and shape remind me

of the cho-cho in Grandma's Saturday Soup.

Grandma tells me about de fruits in Jamaica.
"In Jamaica yu can walk to school and pick a piece a fruit
from a tree, a ripe mango, all juicy and sweet."

Grandma tells me about the fruits in Jamaica.

"In Jamaica you can walk to school and pick a piece of fruit

from a tree, a ripe mango all juicy and sweet."

After school, as a treat fi good marks, Mummy and Daddy tek me go a cinema.
When we get deh de sun was shining, but it was still cold.
I think spring time is coming.

After school, as a treat for good marks, Mum and Dad took me to the cinema.

When we got there the sun was shining, but it was still cold.

I think springtime is coming.

De film was great and wen we came out de sun was setting over de town.
As it set it was big and orange jus' like de pumpkin inna Grandma's Saturday Soup.

The film was great and when we came out the sun was setting over the town.
As it set it was big and orange just like the pumpkin in Grandma's Saturday Soup.

Grandma tells me about de sunrise and sunsets in Jamaica.
"De sun rises early and meks you feel good and ready fi de day."

Grandma tells me about the sunrise and sunsets in Jamaica.
"The sun rises early and makes you feel good and ready for your day."

"*When it sets and de moon comes out she is followed by a million stars dat look like diamonds twinkling inna de nite sky.*"
A million stars, I cyannt imagin' dat many.

"*When it sets and the moon comes out she is followed by a million stars that look like diamonds twinkling in the night sky.*"
A million stars, I can't even imagine that many.

Saturday mornin' I went to my dance class.
De music was slow and sad.

Saturday morning I went to my dance class. The music was slow and sad.

Grandma tells me about de riddims of calypso music and steel pans, of people playin' under de shade of a tree. A wonderful tree with long leaves dat look like de strands of skin from a green banana.
"De music makes you happy and want fi dance."

Grandma tells me about the rhythms of calypso music and steel drums, of people playing under the shade of a tree. A wonderful tree with long leaves that look like the strands of skin from a green banana.
"The music makes you happy and want to dance."

Mummy picked me up after class. We went by car.
We drove down de road and pas' my school. We turned left at de park and on pas' de library. Through de town, there's de cinema and not much further now.

Mum picked me up after class. We went by car.

We drove down the road and past my school. We turned left at the park and on past the

library. Through the town, there's the cinema and not much further now.

I was hungry. Really hungry. At last we arrive at Grandma's.

I was hungry. Really hungry. At last we arrived at Grandma's.

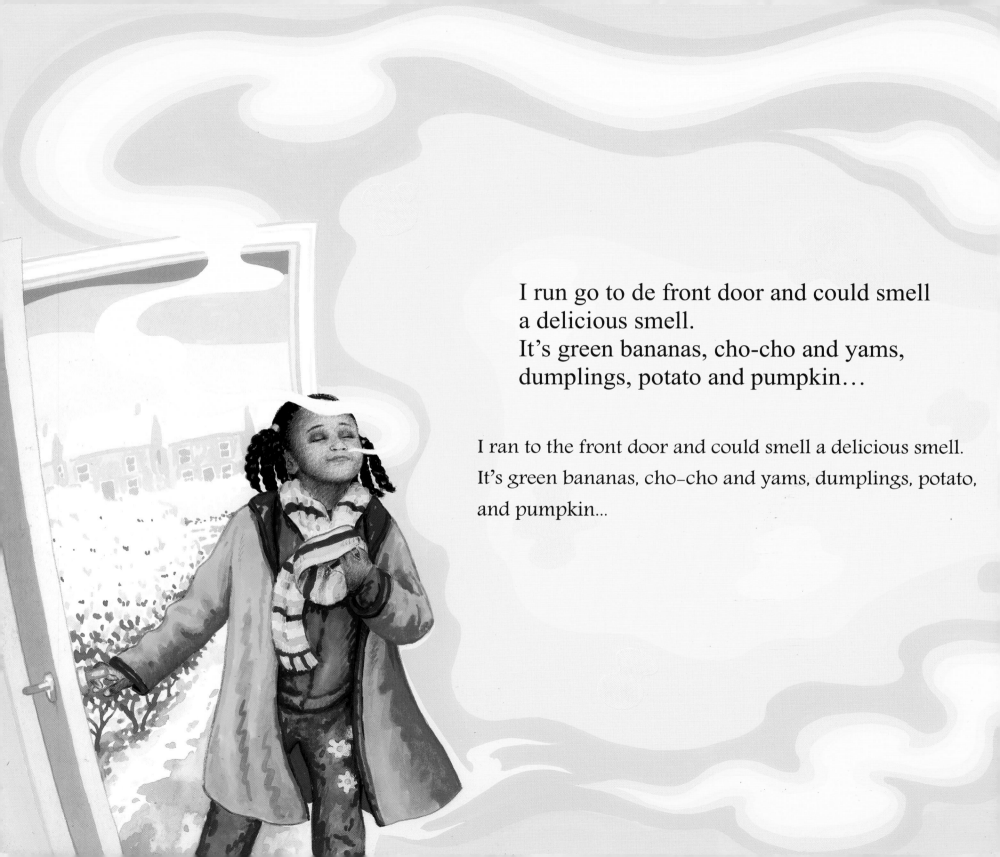

I run go to de front door and could smell
a delicious smell.
It's green bananas, cho-cho and yams,
dumplings, potato and pumpkin…

I ran to the front door and could smell a delicious smell.

It's green bananas, cho-cho and yams, dumplings, potato,

and pumpkin…

spring onions, chicken, a good pinch of Grandma's country seasoning and a lotta chicken stock.
It's Grandma's Saturday Soup!

spring onions, chicken, a good pinch of Grandma's country seasoning and a lot of chicken stock.

It's Grandma's Saturday Soup!

On Sunday we had friends at our house fi dinner.
Mummy and Daddy are good cooks, dem food is nice, but my
favourite food in de whole wide world is Grandma's Saturday Soup.

On **Sunday** we had friends at our house for dinner.
Mum and Dad are good cooks, their food is nice but my favourite
food in the whole wide world is **Grandma's Saturday Soup.**